TROUBLE at TABLE 5

#4:
I Can't Feel My Feet

Check out all the

books!

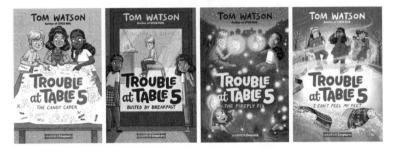

#1   #2   #3   #4

Read more books by **Tom Watson**

#1-12   #1-5

HARPER Chapters

TROUBLE at TABLE 5

#4:
I Can't Feel My Feet

by **Tom Watson**

illustrated by
Marta Kissi

HARPER
An Imprint of HarperCollins*Publishers*

Dedicated to MEJ
(TFLAMSJ)

Library of Congress Control Number: 2020943163
ISBN 978-0-06-295350-6 — ISBN 978-0-06-295349-0 (pbk.)

Typography by Torborg Davern
20 21 22 23 24   PC/LSCC   10 9 8 7 6 5 4 3 2 1
❖
First Edition

Table of Contents

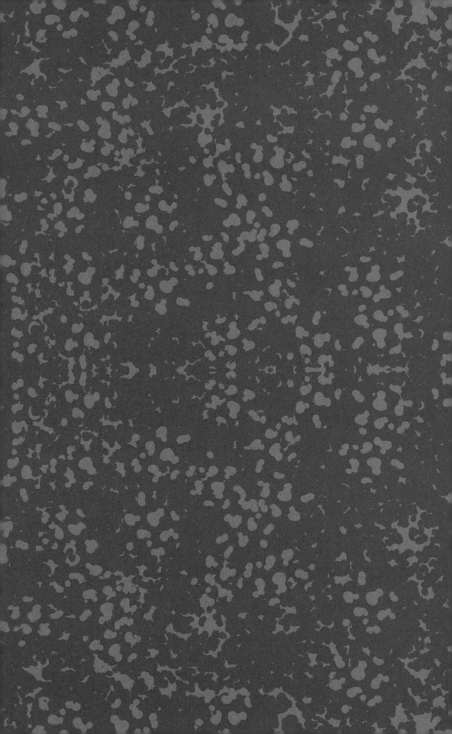

CHAPTER ONE
I CAN'T FEEL MY FEET

❄ 28° F

IT WAS FRIDAY. It was cold. Super cold.

The sidewalk was covered in cold, gray slush as Rosie, Simon, and I walked to school. It had snowed the past couple of days and now it was all melty and clumpy.

There were 412 sidewalk squares from the end of my driveway to the front door of school.

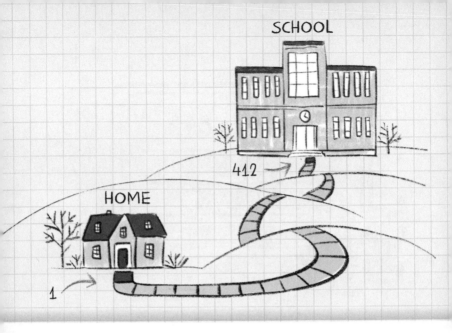

I had counted them, like, a million times.

I couldn't count them that morning though, because of the slush. It was fine. I already knew there were 412. And it was an even number—I like things that are even numbers.

So instead of counting the sidewalk squares as we walked and talked, I stayed busy being cold.

"It's cold," I said.

"It's freezing," Simon confirmed and shivered his shoulders. "I checked the thermometer on our garage. It said twenty-eight degrees. And Mom said it's going to get even colder the next few days. The high on Monday is supposed to be thirteen degrees."

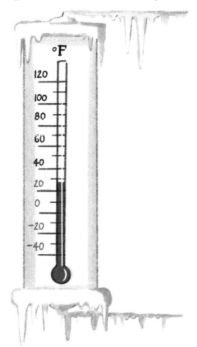

"Thirteen will be the *high* temperature?!" I asked.

Simon nodded. His nose and cheeks were already bright pink and we weren't even halfway to school yet.

"What's the low going to be?" Rosie asked.

"You don't want to know," Simon said, shoving his hands deep in his pockets. He found a dime, pulled it out, and looked at it for a second. He seemed really excited about it for some reason. Then he pushed his hands back into his pockets to get warm.

"You can tell us," Rosie said. "How cold?"

"Eight degrees."

"Maybe it will snow more," I said hopefully. "Maybe we'll have a snow day

and not have to walk to school when it's freezing."

"I thought of that too, Molly," Simon told me. We could see the school in the distance now. "But Mom said there wasn't any snow in the forecast. Just cold. Then colder. Then on Monday, coldest."

Rosie groaned and pulled her knitted hat down over her ears. Her hat had one of those fuzzy balls on top that jiggled as she pulled it down.

5

She said, "I can't feel my feet."

"Me neither," Simon agreed.

We quickened our pace. By the time we got to school, we were practically running. It wasn't a fun kind of running. It was more like a we-don't-want-to-be-outside-one-more-second kind of running.

CHAPTER TWO

ROSIE TWIRLS, SIMON DIGS

WE GOT TO class early because we hustled on the walk to school. We took our regular seats at Table 5 and Rosie started twirling her hair right away. I knew that meant she was thinking hard about something.

Simon and I both wondered why. I didn't ask her. I didn't want to interrupt. But Simon doesn't care about things like that.

He just says whatever he wants—whenever he wants. That's the way he operates.

"What are you thinking about?" he asked as he dug around in the bottom of his backpack.

Rosie turned to him. She stopped twirling her hair.

"It will be eight degrees on Monday," Rosie whispered. Her face turned kind of

stern and serious-looking. "I don't want to be cold walking to school. We have to figure out a way to stay warm."

"We can't control the weather," Simon said, still digging.

"What are you looking for?" I asked.

"Money," he answered. "Sometimes coins fall to the bottom of my backpack."

"Did you forget your lunch money?" Rosie asked.

"No, I packed today," Simon said. "My dad's birthday is coming up and I have a cool idea for a gift. But it's expensive."

"What's your idea?" I asked.

"Tickets to a monster truck show," he answered as he pulled his hand out of the backpack. "Bad news—no coins. But I have good news for you, Rosie."

"What's that?"

"I have some ideas for how to stay warm on the way to school."

"Really?" Rosie asked. She sounded a little excited. She definitely didn't want to be cold on Monday morning. "Let's hear them."

We were glad class hadn't started. Mr. Willow was writing the day's schedule and other stuff on the whiteboard.

That usually took a few minutes. When he was done, that's when class officially started and we had to get totally quiet.

Simon had plenty of ideas. And once he got going, he really got going.

"First, we could just move," Simon suggested. "You know, closer to the equator. Maybe to the rain forest. Or a desert or something. I mean, if we want to be warmer in the winter, we should just go to a place that doesn't have winter."

"Umm," Rosie said and paused. "I don't think our parents will move just because we're cold walking to school."

Simon nodded. He seemed to have already thought of this.

"Okay, I have a couple of other ideas," Simon said. He started to talk faster. "I was thinking about the warmest place in our house. It's by the fireplace. And I thought we could use that."

"Use your fireplace?" I asked as I looked toward the front of the classroom. Mr. Willow was halfway done with the schedule.

"No, just the fire part," Simon explained. "We could each get a log and light one end on fire. As we walk to school, we poke the fire end at each other. Wave it around real close! Toasty!"

1. DESERT

2. FIRE

13

"Simon, I don't want to wave fire at my two best friends," I said.

"And wouldn't the fire spread to the other end of the log pretty quickly?" Rosie asked. "Wouldn't it burn our hands?"

Simon scrunched up his face as he considered our points.

"Okay," he said, moving on. "I like my third idea the best anyway."

And that meant trouble at Table 5.

CHAPTER THREE

HERE COMES TROUBLE

"WHAT'S YOUR THIRD idea?" Rosie asked.

"Do you remember my Halloween costume last year?"

Rosie and I both nodded. Simon had been a muscleman in a big rubber inflatable suit. It was super fun watching him bounce into trees and mailboxes and stuff without getting hurt.

"We should all get muscleman suits," he said quickly. His voice got louder, his words came out faster, and he sort of bounced up and down as he talked.

"We'll inflate the costumes with hair dryers. They trap the hot air inside. I got pretty warm when I was trick-or-treating—and that was a really cold night."

Mr. Willow finished writing the schedule. He stood in front of his desk waiting for everyone to get quiet.

Rosie and I noticed.

Simon did not.

"We keep the hair dryers going all the way to school," Simon said, continuing with his idea. "It will be totally warm. I mean, we might be sweating by the time we get here! I bet we could wear shorts inside the muscleman suits!"

Mr. Willow clicked his tongue behind his teeth. Everybody got quiet—except Simon.

CLASS SCHEDULE

READING
SCIENCE
HISTORY

Rosie and I nodded toward the front of class. But Simon misunderstood us.

"I'm glad you both like my idea!" Simon said. Then he just did what he always does—he kept talking. "We have to keep the hair dryers going and it's almost a mile to school. So we'll need lots of extension cords. We'll plug them into each other—like Christmas lights!"

TABLE
5

Rosie wanted to tell Simon his idea was crazy—you can't drag electrical cords through snow and slush.

We wanted to tell him everybody else was quiet. And class was starting. And Mr. Willow was staring at him.

But we weren't allowed to talk.

Only Mr. Willow could talk.

"Simon!" Mr. Willow said loudly.

19

"Ee-ack!" Simon squealed and jumped in his seat. His chair jerked backward. Lots of people laughed. It wasn't mean. They just saw Simon being Simon.

"Yes?! Yes, Mr. Willow?"

"Why are you talking about Christmas lights?"

"You heard that?"

"We all heard it," Mr. Willow said. He sighed and shook his head. "The classes at the end of the hall heard it."

"Sorry," Simon said. "I was jus—"

"I don't need to know," Mr. Willow said and raised his hand toward Simon.

"I'd rather get our day going. Before we get started, does anyone have questions about what we worked on yesterday?"

Rosie shot her left hand up in the air.

"Yes, Rosie?" Mr. Willow said and smiled. He didn't like Simon talking when he shouldn't. But he did like it when Rosie had a good, smart question.

"It's not from yesterday though," Rosie admitted. "Is that okay?"

"That's okay."

"Mr. Willow," she said, "what are some different ways to generate heat?"

THREE CHAPTERS DOWN! HOW WOULD YOU ANSWER ROSIE'S QUESTION?

CHAPTER FOUR

ROSIE'S
GOT IT

WE DIDN'T WANT to go outside at the end of the school day, but we had to walk home.

It already felt colder.

As we trudged through the slush, we talked about the different heat-generating ideas that Mr. Willow told us about. Would any of them help us on the super cold walk to school Monday morning?

"We need to go nuclear!" Simon exclaimed. "We can dig up some uranium. Mr. Willow said uranium gets hot if you break it up or something."

Rosie said, "It's called nuclear fission."

"Yeah, we'll do some fission-y stuff," Simon said. "We can get some chunks of uranium and just stick them in our pockets or whatever."

"Umm, I don't think we should expose ourselves to nuclear energy," I said.

"Why not?"

"It's totally dangerous," Rosie answered. "We'd be radioactive! We'd be sick! We'd glow in the dark!"

"Sounds kind of fun, doesn't it?"

"No!" Rosie and I yelled and laughed.

"All right, all right," Simon said. "What else did Mr. Willow say?"

"Electromagnetic radiation," Rosie said. "Like from a microwave oven."

"Why don't we just get a huge microwave oven?" Simon suggested. "Get inside, turn it on, and travel to school in it somehow. We can use the wagon in my garage."

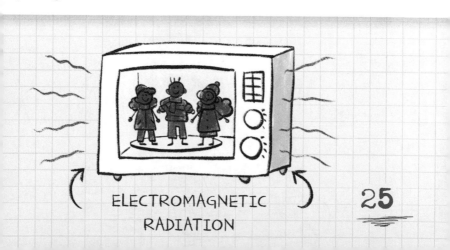

ELECTROMAGNETIC
RADIATION

25

Even though it was really cold and we wanted to get home, Rosie stopped on the sidewalk. Simon and I stopped too.

"You want us to cook ourselves?" Rosie asked.

Simon nodded. "We'd be warm."

"We'd be dinner!" she screamed.

"I bet I'd taste the best," Simon replied.

We started walking again. I could see my house. Mom was all bundled up and in the front yard. She was covering her rosebushes like she does every winter.

"Mr. Willow also said friction makes heat," Rosie reminded us. "Like rubbing two sticks together to make fire."

"You know what makes great fire?" Simon asked, getting excited. "The Raging Inferno monster truck! It shoots fire out of its exhaust pipe! It's awesome!"

"I don't mean actually making fire," Rosie responded quickly. She wanted to stay on the subject. We both knew Simon could talk a *loooong* time about monster trucks. "I mean just rubbing something together to create heat."

Rosie stopped again when we got to my driveway. Simon and I did too.

She raised her hands and rubbed them

together as she said, "Friction."

Simon and I watched her. I could tell she was working something out. She stretched the mitten on her left hand. Rosie then took the mitten off and brought it up close to her eyes. She examined it.

"Umm, nice mitten," Simon said. "But I'm freezing my butt off. Can we go now?"

"The cotton has holes in it," Rosie said, ignoring him. "But it still traps the heat from my hand."

She put her mitten back on and looked toward my house. I think she was looking at my mom.

"Just a reminder," Simon said. He wanted to get moving. "Butt. Freezing. Off."

Rosie smiled and said, "I figured it out."

"Awesome!" I said and shivered. "Tell us inside. We'll make hot chocolate."

CHAPTER FIVE

MARSHMALLOWS AND FRICTION

❄ 15° F

WE DIDN'T USE the hot chocolate mix that comes in an envelope and you just add hot water. We made the good hot chocolate—with real milk. Mom poured the milk into a pot and set it on the stove.

"You guys can take it from here," Mom said after she turned on the burner. "I need to get back to my rosebushes."

"Why do you cover them up?" Simon asked.

"To protect them from the wind and the cold," Mom answered as she pulled her gloves back on. "They'll bloom better in the spring if they're covered with burlap in the winter. And I have to get it done— it's going to be *so* cold on Monday."

Mom went to work on her rosebushes, and we worked on the hot chocolate.

Rosie squirted the chocolate syrup into

the pot. Simon did the stirring. And I got a bag of marshmallows from the cabinet. They were the little ones, not the big giant ones.

"So how are we going to stay warm on Monday?" Simon asked Rosie.

"We're going to use friction—and trap the heat," Rosie said.

Simon and I had no idea what Rosie's plan was, but we totally trusted her.

After the chocolate milk got hot, we poured it into three mugs and sat at the kitchen table. Rosie put a few marshmallows into her mug.

Simon grabbed a big handful and dropped them in his mug. A couple overflowed, but he just ate them straightaway.

I used six marshmallows (an even number). But they got melty pretty fast, so I needed to scoop them out two (another even number) at a time to eat them. I didn't want them to melt into one (an odd number) big marshmallowy blob.

"What's your plan?" Simon asked, taking a slow, careful sip of hot chocolate.

After that sip, there was a little more room in his mug, so he dropped in some more marshmallows.

"We're going to make our own heat on the way to school," Rosie started to explain. She rubbed her hands together to remind us what friction means. "And we're going to trap it like inside a mitten."

"What are we going to rub together?" I asked.

"We need to figure that out after we drink our hot chocolate," Rosie said.

That was enough explanation for Simon and me. We were confident Rosie knew what to do.

The hot chocolate was cool enough to drink instead of sip now. Simon gulped half of his down in two big swallows. Then he filled his mug to the top with marshmallows.

"Simon!" Rosie exclaimed.

"What?"

"You have more marshmallows than hot chocolate!"

He brought the mug up and tilted his head back, and lots of marshmallows and a little hot chocolate flowed into his mouth. He looked at us— his mouth was so full that he couldn't close it.

He said, "I wuv marf-ma-woes!"

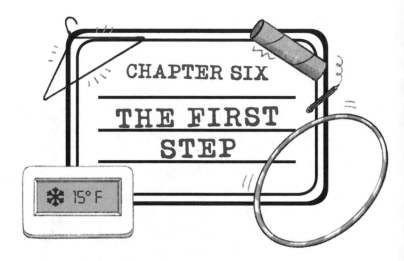

CHAPTER SIX

THE FIRST STEP

❄ 15° F

WE FINISHED OUR hot chocolate and Rosie got all sciencey.

"First, we need to find out what material will get the hottest when we rub it," Rosie explained. "We need to test paper, wood, metal, and plastic."

We got a pencil (wood), a paper towel tube (paper), a coat hanger (metal), and my Hula-Hoop (plastic). We put them all on the kitchen table.

"This isn't quite right for our experiment," Rosie said as she held the pencil up and looked at it. She scratched at its surface with her fingernail. "It's painted. We need to get to the wood underneath."

"Let me try," Simon said.

Rosie handed it to him. Then Simon put the pencil in his  mouth and started to scrape it against his teeth.

"Don't do that!" Rosie exclaimed and held her hand out to get the pencil back.

"Why not?" Simon asked, giving it back to her.

"You might swallow some paint!"

Simon just shrugged. Rosie shook her head at him. It wasn't mean. She just thought he was crazy.

"I'll get some sandpaper," I said. "We have some in the basement."

We took turns rubbing the paint off the pencil with the sandpaper. It came off fast.

"Okay," I said when all the paint was rubbed off the pencil. "What now?"

Rosie showed us what we needed to do. We each took turns rubbing the objects—the pencil, Hula-Hoop, hanger, and paper towel tube—between our thumbs and pointer fingers. We rubbed them real fast for about fifteen seconds.

We wanted to find out which one got the hottest.

Rosie asked us not to share our answers. She said that could influence the results.

"Okay," Rosie said after we tested each one. "Which one got hottest?"

"It wasn't even close," Simon said. "It was the coat hanger."

"Totally," I said. "It almost burned my finger."

Rosie nodded and smiled. I could tell that was her result too. And I think she already knew the metal hanger would get hottest. She just wanted to confirm it with a scientific test.

I reached out and touched the hanger.

"It's still warm," I said.

Rosie nodded and smiled. She knew it would still be warm.

43

"So," Simon said and looked at Rosie, "we're going to walk to school rubbing coat hangers the whole time? Our hands will get pretty tired—and hot."

Rosie glanced down at the stuff on the table and twirled her hair.

"We're not going to use coat hangers," Rosie said and looked at us both. "And we're not going to walk."

CHAPTER SEVEN

SIMON'S SEARCH

ROSIE WAS BUSY with the Math Fair all day Saturday. Simon had basketball practice at noon on Sunday. So we didn't meet up until Sunday afternoon. By that time, it wasn't slushy on the sidewalk anymore—it was icy.

We met Simon at his garage to get started. We checked the thermometer outside the door before going in.

"It's fifteen degrees," I said.

Simon yelled, "It's going to be even colder tomorrow!"

He had to yell because he was inside his mom's car. We could see him through the windshield. All the car doors were open.

"Why are you in there?" Rosie called.

"I'm trying to go to the big monster truck show in Chicago with my dad!" Simon called back and then scrunched down out of sight. "Remember? For his birthday."

This explanation made, umm, no sense to Rosie and me.

We hurried into the garage and looked inside the car. Simon was in the back seat. Both of his arms were shoved elbow-deep into the back-seat cushion.

"Simon, *what* are you doing?" Rosie asked. She tried not to laugh.

"The monster truck show," Simon said and grunted, pushing his arms even deeper. "For Dad."

"How is shoving your arms into the back seat of your mom's car going to get you to a monster truck show in Chicago?" Rosie asked.

"The tickets are expensive," Simon explained, still pushing and grunting.

"And Dad's birthday is in two weeks."

"But Simon, why are you—?" Rosie said and mimicked him, pushing her arms forward in the air and grunting.

"I need money to buy the tickets," he answered. "They're twenty-five dollars apiece. I need to get fifty dollars."

"In your mom's car?" I asked.

"Sometimes you can find money in here," Simon explained. He squeezed his eyes shut and searched with his fingers. "Coins fall out of people's pockets and go down into the seats."

"Simon," Rosie said. "To find fifty dollars in coins, you'd have to—"

Simon interrupted Rosie.

"Aha!" he yelled and yanked his hands out. He held up a quarter for Rosie and me to see. "Jackpot!"

"Only forty-nine dollars and seventy-five cents to go," Rosie said.

"Not that much," Simon replied as he climbed awkwardly out of the car. He pulled some more coins from his pocket. "I found some in the front seat too. And in the cushions of the living room couch!

And in my jeans on Friday."

We couldn't tell exactly how much money Simon had, but we knew it wasn't anywhere near fifty dollars.

Right then a freezing gust of air blew in through the garage door. Simon rushed to close it. That bitter-cold air blast reminded us why we were there.

"Okay," Rosie said and rubbed her hands together. "We better get started."

CHAPTER EIGHT

TIME TO START

SIMON'S DAD HAD parked his car in the driveway for us so we'd have plenty of room to build our project.

"We have to get this done before we walk to school tomorrow morning. That doesn't give us much time," Rosie said and shivered. "Let's get moving. That will warm us up some. Thanks for bringing the burlap, Molly."

"Mom said we can use as much as we want," I said and dropped it on the concrete floor.

"What else do we need?" Simon asked. "Please tell me we don't have to go outside to get anything."

"We only need one thing from your house," Rosie said and smiled. "But we don't need it until the end. Everything else is in here."

So we got everything we needed and put it all with the roll of burlap.

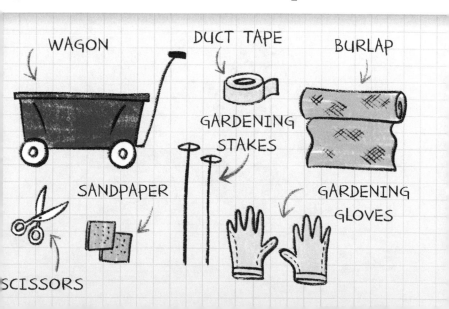

"Let's make sure two of us can fit inside the wagon first," Rosie said. "And that each of us can pull the other two."

So we did that.

Rosie and I got in the wagon. We sat facing each other. Simon pulled us around the garage. Then Rosie pulled Simon and me. And then I pulled Rosie and Simon.

"Okay, there's plenty of room," Rosie said when we were done. "And we are all strong enough to pull the other two. I'm

sorry only two of us will be warm."

"That's better than all three of us being cold," I said to Rosie. "Plus, we'll take turns each day."

"I want to pull you two on the first day," Simon volunteered quickly.

"Why?" I asked.

"You'll see," Simon said and grinned.

"I thought we'd play rock, paper, scissors to decide," Rosie said.

"Nope," Simon said. "I'll pull first."

"Okay," Rosie said. She picked up the metal gardening stakes and the duct tape.

And we got to work.

We stood up two metal stakes in the wagon about a third of the way in from each end. They were wobbly, but we used a ton of duct tape to hold them in place. Rosie said when the burlap was over them, that would help too.

And she was right.

We draped the burlap over the poles and the wagon. Then we used scissors to cut it so it ended halfway down the wagon's sides. As we did, Simon made a suggestion.

"I think we need a name," he said.

"For the wagon?" I asked.

"For the whole thing," Simon said. "I mean, we're transforming this thing. It's not a wagon anymore. It's a whole new invention."

"We should name it after Rosie," I said. "It's all her idea. Or paint a message along the side or something."

"No, not after me," Rosie said modestly. "It's all of us working together."

"The Rosie Rocket!" Simon yelled, ignoring her.

YOU'VE READ EIGHT CHAPTERS AND 3,792 WORDS. YOU'RE MAKING GREAT PROGRESS!

CHAPTER NINE

ROSIE-DOZY-DING-DONG

ROSIE SHOOK HER head at Simon's name suggestion.

But that didn't stop him. Simon kept shouting names as we worked—and Rosie shook her head after each one.

We used more duct tape to secure the bottom edges of the burlap all along the wagon's sides. It was starting to look like a sagging, badly shaped bubble.

"Raging Rosie!" Simon exclaimed. "Like the Raging Inferno monster truck!"

It took a little time to tape the front by the wagon handle, but we figured it out.

"Rosie's Winter Wagon!"

Rosie and I made a vertical cut in the burlap at the back of the wagon. That was how we would get in.

While we did that, Simon tested some sandpaper on a gardening stake that we didn't use. He wanted to see if it got warm like the coat hanger had.

"Whoa!" Simon said when he touched the metal. "This thing is hot!"

"That's why we'll wear the gardening gloves," Rosie said. "They're rubbery on the palms, so we won't burn our hands."

We poked holes along both sides of the back seam.

"We need to close up this seam," Rosie said and twirled her hair.

"I'm on it," Simon said and went over to a cardboard box against the wall. Rosie and I knew what was in there—a bunch of his old, beat-up sneakers. When we cleaned the garage in the summer, Simon wouldn't let us throw them away.

"You're going to let us use your *sneakers*?" Rosie asked, surprised. "But what about all your special memories?"

Simon hadn't let us throw them away because he remembered doing certain things in each pair. He *loved* his sneakers.

"Not the sneakers," Simon said, bringing two pairs. "Just the shoelaces."

As we took the laces out, Simon told us what was special about each pair.

"I caught a wicked garter snake when I was wearing the black ones," he said. "It was green with a yellow stripe."

"What about the red ones?" Rosie asked.

"With those, I slipped on a wet rock down by the creek and cracked my head against another rock," Simon said casually. "It didn't hurt that much, but I got a bad cut. And I had a lot of blood on my cheek."

"*That's* a special memory?" I asked. We had the laces out now.

"No, that's not the special part."

Rosie asked, "What is?"

"When Mom saw all the blood, she felt sorry for me," Simon answered. "She got me some gelato for the first time. Have you guys had gelato? It's delicious! It's way better than ice cream!"

"So, umm, bashing your head against a rock was worth it because you got to have gelato?" I asked.

"Totally."

We tied the flaps with the shoelaces.

"One more step," Rosie said, looking at the wagon. "We need a hair dryer."

"Rosie-Dozy-Ding-Dong!" Simon shouted.

CHAPTER TEN

PUFFING UP

❄ 10° F

SIMON BROUGHT HIS mom's hair dryer into the garage. We plugged it into an extension cord—and plugged that cord into the wall.

"We should run through all the steps like it's tomorrow morning," Rosie suggested.

"You two hop in," Simon said as we untied the shoelaces on the burlap flaps. "I'm going to be pulling tomorrow."

"I can't believe it's going to be *even*

colder in the morning," I said as I got into the wagon.

"I really hope this works," Rosie said, climbing in after me.

Simon tied the flap shut—except for the very top. That's where he stuck the end of the hair dryer.

He turned it on.

"Rosa-Pa-Looza!" he shouted.

After being in the cold garage for so long, that blast of hot air felt awesome.

Rosie and I took turns holding our hands up to it.

It took about three minutes for it to feel pretty warm inside the burlap bubble. It didn't blow up like a balloon or anything because burlap has lots of tiny holes in it. But it did stop sagging a bit.

"Okay, Simon!" Rosie yelled over the

loud hair dryer. "You can turn it off now!"

He turned off the hair dryer, pulled it out, and tied the final shoelace. We knew the warm air would escape, but we wanted it to be as slow as possible.

"What do we do now?" I asked.

"We wait," Rosie said. "I want to see how long this holds the warm air."

While we waited inside, Simon worked on the outside. He felt all around and added extra duct tape wherever he thought warm air might be escaping.

"Warm and Cozy Rosie!"

It didn't take long for the burlap to start sagging—just a few minutes. And it was already colder inside.

"You can let us out now," Rosie said.

Simon untied and opened the flaps.

"That didn't last too long," Simon said. You could hear a little disappointment in his voice.

"Yeah," I said as Rosie and I climbed out. I was a little bummed with the result too. "It takes fifteen minutes to get to school and it only took a couple minutes for the air to cool down."

"It's okay," Rosie said and smiled. She tossed the gardening gloves and sandpaper into the wagon. "The hair dryer just gives us a head start. We're going to generate our own heat on the way using friction. The burlap will protect us some from the wind.

HAIR DRYER

WARM AIR

GARDENING STAKES

BURLAP

HANDLE

WAGON

EXTENSION CORD

71

And we'll be moving around when we rub the stakes. All of that will help us stay warm."

This made me and Simon feel better. We trusted Rosie—and liked her confidence.

"We'll find out for sure tomorrow morning," I said. Rosie and I zipped up our coats and got ready to go back outside. Simon climbed back into his mom's car to look for more coins.

"I have an idea," Rosie whispered to me as we pulled on our mittens. "To help Simon."

But she didn't tell me her idea until we got outside. That's because right then, Simon shouted something from the car.

It was something I don't think he's ever said before.

"I can't wait to go to school tomorrow!"

ONLY TWO MORE CHAPTERS TO GO. HOW DO YOU THINK THEIR PLAN WILL TURN OUT?

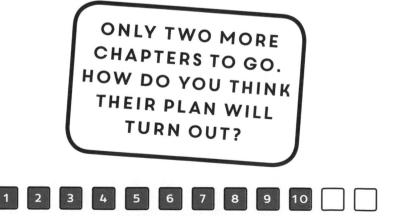

❄ 10° F

ON MONDAY MORNING we got to Simon's garage fifteen minutes early. Rosie and I ran almost the whole way. It was super cold *and* we couldn't wait to test the wagon.

The thermometer read ten degrees.

Simon was waiting for us in the garage.

"Check this out," Simon said and pointed to the side of the wagon. You could tell he was proud of something. Along the side of the wagon, Simon had painted the name of the invention.

"Awesome, right?" Simon yelled.

Rosie and I laughed. I'm not sure Rosie wanted to brag and have her name on the side, but I also think she felt proud of her invention. So I think it was okay.

We put our backpacks in the wagon through the flap at the back. Simon's was already inside. Then Rosie and I climbed in and Simon tied all the shoelaces except for the top one. Then he ran back to his house to get the hair dryer.

"How many tickets did you make?" Rosie asked me.

CATCH A WARM RIDE!
—ADMIT ONE—
TO AND FROM SCHOOL!
$2

"About twenty," I said and patted my backpack.

"Me too."

"He's going to be surprised," I said and

shivered. "I hope he hurries."

"Do you want to start with the rubbing?" Rosie suggested. "That will warm us up some."

It totally did.

We put on the gardening gloves, picked up the sandpaper, and started to rub it against the metal poles. We rubbed faster and faster. We moved that sandpaper up and down for almost a full minute.

Then we stopped to rest and took the gloves off to test the temperature of the metal. It was really warm. I could feel the heat a few inches away from the metal. It was like holding my hands up to a fireplace.

Rosie smiled.

For a minute, I thought that she smiled because the whole rubbing-the-metal-pole-heat-generating-friction thing had worked to perfection.

But that wasn't what she was smiling at.

Simon had come back into the garage.

She pointed at him—and laughed.

I turned to see. It took me a few seconds to figure out what I was looking at. We could see through the burlap, but it was kind of blurry.

Simon was wearing his muscleman costume from Halloween. The only difference was that he wore his winter coat and hat too. And he was carrying the hair dryer.

He waddled up to us.

"What are you doing?!" Rosie yelled and laughed at the same time.

"I told you I got really warm in this thing on Halloween," Simon yelled back as he plugged the hair dryer into the extension cord. They didn't really need to yell, but it helped since we were separated by the burlap. "Plus, I look totally cool, right? I mean, I look like this super strong guy pulling you two in Rosie's Wicked Ride. Right?!"

We didn't stop laughing until Simon

was done with the hair dryer. Then he tied the final shoelace. He pulled us down the driveway, past his dad's car, and onto the sidewalk. We saw his mom and dad taking pictures of us from inside the house.

Rosie and I put on the gardening gloves and picked up the sandpaper.

It was time to heat things up.

CHAPTER TWELVE

CLAPPING AND HONKING

❄ 8°F

IT TOOK ABOUT fifteen minutes to get to school.

And Rosie and I were totally warm—for lots of reasons.

1. Rosie's Wicked Ride was warmed up to begin with by the hair dryer.

2. We were protected from the wind.

3. Rubbing the metal poles with the sandpaper totally worked. They got hot— and warmed the air inside. Every few

minutes, we rubbed them again to keep them hot.

4. The activity itself warmed us up too. We weren't just sitting there. You know what I mean?

It was fun.

And it was something else too.

It was entertaining.

Not for us.

For other people.

I mean, how often do you see a muscleman pulling a burlap-wrapped-bubble-wagon thing down the sidewalk? And inside there are two girls frantically rubbing sandpaper up and down two metal poles?

Umm, not very often.

If ever.

It was a rare and unique thing to see. So when people saw it, they stared.

They yelled.

They clapped.

They whistled.

Cars drove alongside us and honked.

Not like loud, blaring, mean honks. It wasn't like this: *HOOOOOOOOONK!* It was more like short, friendly, encouraging honks, like this: *Beep! Beep!*

It was crazy.

It was fun.

And it was warm.

"I think we can stop now," Rosie suggested once we turned a corner on the sidewalk and saw the school.

"I know we all worked together and everything," I said and stopped rubbing. "But I'm glad Simon painted *Rosie's Wicked Ride* along the side. It was your idea."

"Thanks," she said. And then she changed the subject. I knew she would. She doesn't like to take credit for stuff. That's just the way she is. She asked, "Do you think we should give Simon the tickets right away?"

"Let's wait until we get inside," I answered. "We'll give them to him at Table 5."

And that's what we did.

TABLE
5

HIGH FIVE!

You've read **12** chapters,

87 pages,

and **5,686** words!

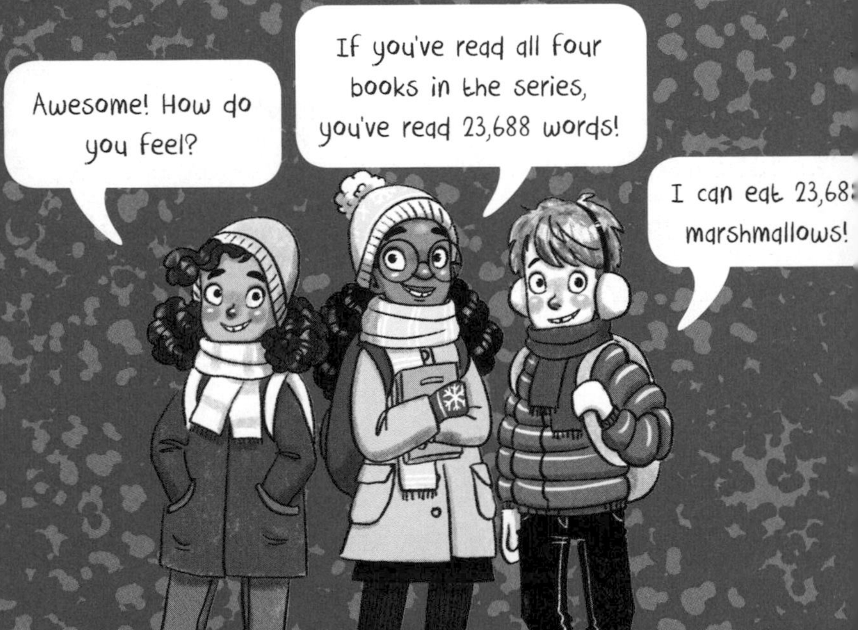

Fun and Games!

THINK

In this book, Rosie, Molly, and Simon solve the problem of staying warm on their walk to school. Can you invent a contraption that helps you solve a problem at your house? Maybe you'll invent something that lots of other kids can use too!

FEEL

How does a really cold day make you feel? What about a really hot day? What do you like most about each? Snowball fights? Playing in the sprinkler? If you had to choose, would you pick a super cold day or a super hot day?

ACT

Try copying Rosie's experiment about friction. Find things that are made out of plastic, metal, paper, and wood. Rub each one real fast. Which object got warmest? Don't burn yourself!

Tom Watson is the author of the popular STICK DOG and STICK CAT series. And now he's the author of this new series, TROUBLE AT TABLE 5. Tom lives in Chicago with his wife and kids and their big dog, Shadow. When he's not at home, Tom's usually out visiting classrooms all over the country. He's met a lot of students who remind him of Molly, Simon, and Rosie. He's learned that kids are smarter than adults. Like, way smarter.

Marta Kissi is originally from Warsaw but now lives in London where she loves bringing stories to life. She shares her art studio with her husband, James, and their pet plant, Trevor.